Ju
F
H42   Herman, Charlotte.
              The house on Walenska
         Street.

Temple Israel Library
Minneapolis, Minn.

Please sign your full name on the above
card.

Return books promptly to the Library or
Temple Office.

Fines will be charged for overdue books
or for damage or loss of same.

THE HOUSE
ON WALENSKA STREET

OTHER BOOKS BY CHARLOTTE HERMAN

THE HOUSE
ON WALENSKA STREET

by Charlotte Herman

illustrated by Susan Avishai

E. P. DUTTON · NEW YORK

With gratitude to my aunt Esther Levinson, for continuing the story my mother began. And to my cousin Reid Simmons, for the Liss Family Tree.

Library of Congress Cataloging-in-Publication Data

Herman, Charlotte.
   The house on Walenska Street / by Charlotte Herman.
     p. cm.
   Summary: Relates the experiences of eight-year-old Leah, her two younger sisters, and their widowed mother living in a small Russian town in 1913.
   ISBN 0-525-44519-6
   [1. Jews—Soviet Union—Fiction. 2. Family life—Fiction.]
   I. Title.
PZ7.H4313Ho   1990   89-33505
[Fic]—dc20   CIP
                                      AC

Published in the United States by E. P. Dutton, a division of Penguin Books USA Inc.

Published simultaneously in Canada by Fitzhenry & Whiteside Limited, Toronto

Designer: Martha Rago

Printed in the U.S.A.   First Edition
10 9 8 7 6 5 4 3 2 1

for Anna ז״ל
and the three sisters of Walenska Street—

to my aunt Esther, with love,
in memory of my aunt Rose,
and remembering Leah, my mother
C.H.

Contents

CHAPTER 1

"Mama, Come Quick!"

"Mama, come quick! Esther stuck a ribbon in her nose." Leah ran from the bedroom to the kitchen, where Mama was baking bread.

Mama pulled a pan of dark, round Russian rye out of the big baker's oven. She set it on top of the wooden table. "Esther stuck what, where?" she asked.

"A ribbon in her nose," said Leah. "Hurry, Mama, before it goes all the way up to her head."

"*Oy, gevald!*" said Mama, throwing her hands up in the air. "What will I do with that child?"

Mama and Leah ran into the bedroom and stared in horror at six-year-old Esther, who was sitting on the bed with a red ribbon hanging out of one of her nostrils. Leah couldn't believe how Esther got such a long ribbon in her nose.

"Esther!" cried Mama. "You take that *shmatte*, that piece of rag, out of your nose this minute."

"It's just my hair ribbon," said Esther, pulling the ribbon out of her nose and dangling it in front of her. "See?"

"Esther, why do you do such things?" Mama asked. And then, without waiting for an answer, she turned to Leah. "Why weren't you watching her? You're the oldest. I depend on you."

"I can't watch her every second, Mama. And besides, I had to put Rose to bed. She wanted me to sing her a lullaby."

Chubby-cheeked Rose lay sleeping on the bed that she and Esther shared, her arm around a red and gold tea can. Rose, who was only three, loved to play with all sorts of tin cans and boxes, but lately this red and gold tea can was her favorite. It looked like a small treasure chest.

"Come, Esther," said Mama. "You will wash up and help me bake. And Leah, here. *Shreib* a letter." Mama took a pencil and some paper out of the dresser drawer. "Write to the cousins in America. Tell them we are well."

The cousins in America! Leah loved to write to the cousins. And to all the aunts and uncles who would be sharing the letter. She had a whole family in America that she had never met. Some of the relatives used to live nearby, in Kletsk. But they left for America long before Leah was born. Now they lived in a place called Minnesota, far away from this Russian town of Nesvich and the little house at 15 Walenska Street.

3

Leah grabbed her sweater and ran out into the backyard, away from Esther and Rose, away from whatever work had to be done, away to be alone with her thoughts. She sat on the ground against the chestnut tree and began her letter with the date, October 15, 1913. And she wrote in Yiddish—the language that Leah and her family spoke—to Cousin Ruth and her family.

I am writing this letter in the backyard. It's not much of a yard. It's very small, with just a little grass, a chestnut tree, and a wooden shed with a toilet inside. The yard is not at all like the ones across the street where the doctor and other rich people live. Their yards are more like gardens, with apple and cherry trees and beautiful flowers. I have been in the doctor's garden to play with his daughter, Marina, so I know.

Leah went on to tell how hard Mama worked, baking bread to sell and picking

4

potatoes in the fields. And how lonely it had been since Papa died in the spring. *We miss him very much*, she wrote. Then she remembered to add, *But we are well.*

Leah put down her pencil, leaned against the tree, and thought about Papa. When Papa was alive, he wrote letters to the relatives too. Sometimes Leah and Papa would sit at the long wooden table in the kitchen and write their letters together. Papa always helped her with the spelling. Now it was just Leah who wrote the letters. Mama had never learned to read and write. And Esther and Rose hadn't learned yet. Oh, how she wished Papa was sitting beside her this very minute, writing with her again.

She picked up her pencil and continued the letter.

I dreamed that I was in your kitchen. And you had yellow curtains with white flowers. Can you please write back and tell me if I'm right about the curtains? And tell me more

about Minnesota. I can't believe there are ten thousand lakes in Minnesota. We have lakes here too. But just a few—where we sometimes wash our clothes.

Leah knew that Ruth or one of the relatives would write back. Somebody always did. If not Ruth, it was Sarah or Uncle Avraham or one of the aunts. And always they told her how wonderful her letters were. So full of description. So full of feeling. Remarkable for a girl only eight years old.

Leah leaned farther back against the tree. She wrapped her sweater tightly around herself, closed her eyes, and dreamed about the houses that the relatives in America had—with two or even three bedrooms. Leah could not imagine living in a house with so many bedrooms. Her house had just one room, divided by a curtain, and served as a kitchen and a bedroom. Leah and Mama slept in one bed, Esther and Rose in

7

the other. Leah tried to imagine what it would be like to have a bathroom right inside the house, and sinks with running water.

The sun peeked through the branches of the chestnut tree to warm Leah's face. Now she could see the kitchen in Ruth's house, almost touch the yellow curtains with the white flowers. She was almost there, almost . . .

"Leah, Leah!" It was Esther, calling from the window, flour all over her face. "Leah, Rose is up, and Mama wants you to come in."

Leah sighed as she folded the unfinished letter and placed it, with the pencil, in her sweater pocket.

Then she got up and walked slowly toward the house.

CHAPTER 2

Leah Takes
Care of Mama

"Mama, come quick! Esther is stuck in
the window." Leah dropped the comb she
was using for Rose's curls and hurried to
the bedroom window. "Quick, Mama," she
called again as she grabbed Esther by the
arms. "Her front half is inside the house,
and her back half is still outside."

"What now?" Mama came rushing into
the bedroom. She shook her head at the
sight before her.

The window, which swung to the outside,

was opened only partway, leaving a small space. And sticking out of that space, from head to waist, arms in front, was Esther, looking slightly annoyed.

"Esther, how did you get in the window?" Mama tried to force the window all the way open, but it wouldn't budge. She tried to pull Esther inside. Esther wouldn't budge either.

"Mama," said Leah. "I'll go outside and push. You stay inside and pull."

"I go too," said Rose.

Leah and Rose ran outside to the window. While Mama pulled, Leah pushed Esther, and Rose pushed Leah. Esther still wouldn't budge.

Leah and Rose ran back into the house, and Leah heard Esther asking, "Mama, if you can't get the window open, will I have to stay like this forever?"

"We'll get it open," said Mama. "We'll get it open." And she called for Zimmel the shoemaker, who rented a corner of the

kitchen during the day to make his shoes. He had been with them since Papa died. There was no room to work in his house, with his wife and eight children.

"Zimmel," Mama called. "Bring your hammer. And hurry!"

Zimmel was a thin, bearded man who wore a black apron and always seemed to have nails in his mouth. Leah thought that this was probably the reason he didn't talk very much.

Zimmel laughed when he saw Esther. "You look like a *faygeleh*, a little bird who wants to fly but has nowhere to go."

He took his hammer and carefully tapped the top of the window, then the bottom. Gradually it loosened, until it finally swung out to the side. Mama pulled Esther into the bedroom.

Leah danced around the room, singing "Hooray for Zimmel," and Rose clapped her hands and danced with her sister. Zimmel, who was usually very serious, smiled.

Then he placed his hammer on the floor and danced too.

"Tell me, Esther," said Mama, setting Esther on the bed beside her, "were you coming or going?"

"I was playing in the yard," said Esther. "Then I heard horses. I thought the soldiers were coming. So I tried to get in the house."

Leah knew why Esther was frightened of the soldiers. They had both heard about the pogroms, where soldiers or even the towns-people murdered Jews in other towns and villages all over Russia.

Sometimes at night, when Mama and Papa had thought the girls were asleep, they used to speak about the pogroms. Leah and Esther had heard the neighbors talk about them too. Leah herself remembered times the soldiers had come to steal from her family. They had forced their way into the house and taken whatever they wanted— once a silver wine cup that Papa used on

13

the Sabbath and a pair of Mama's copper candlesticks. What if one day the soldiers decided to make a pogrom in Nesvich? She shuddered at the thought.

"I don't think the soldiers are coming today," said Mama.

"Your mama is right," said Zimmel. "We would have gotten word from the neighbors."

Leah hoped the soldiers would never come. Especially now that Papa was gone. When Papa was with them, she had felt protected. Who would protect them now? She thought about Zimmel. She was glad that he was with them. Leah knew that somehow he would protect the family too. But what if the soldiers came when Zimmel was away, delivering shoes? Or at night, after Zimmel had gone?

Mama and Zimmel went back to the kitchen—Zimmel to work on the shoes, and Mama to collect the buckets that were to be filled with water from the well.

"Watch Rose," Leah instructed Esther. "Mama is going to the well." Then, soon after Mama put on her babushka and left, Leah crept after her.

After Papa died, Leah had begun to worry about Mama. She worried that Mama would get sick, like Papa had. Or that her apron would catch on fire when she lit the match for the wood-burning stove. Or that she would fall into the well. So whenever she could, Leah followed her to make sure that didn't happen.

The well was just outside the gate to the park that Leah loved to play in. She hid behind the chestnut and birch trees, far enough back so that Mama wouldn't see her. Leah didn't want Mama to know how worried she was. But when Mama leaned over the well, Leah imagined her falling down, down, deep into the water. And she hurried up close to her.

Mama turned and saw Leah. "Leahla, you came to help?"

15

"Yes, Mama. Maybe I can carry one of the buckets." She watched carefully to make sure that Mama didn't lean over too far. She held on to a corner of Mama's apron.

"It's too heavy for you, Leahla. But you can hold on to the handle, and we will carry it together."

So with Mama carrying one bucket, and Leah helping Mama with the other, they started the walk back to the house. At the door, just before they went in, Mama looked at Leah and smiled.

"Thank you for taking care of me," she said.

CHAPTER 3

A Taste of *Yerissen*

"Mama, come quick! Esther took your jewelry box and she's playing with your locket. I told her to put everything away, but she won't listen to me."

"Esther, you never listen," said Mama, standing near the curtain that separated the kitchen from the bedroom. She had been in the kitchen washing clothes and was wiping her soapy hands on her apron. "How many times do I have to tell you about the jewelry? It is not something to play with."

17

Esther was sitting on the bed, the velvet-lined jewelry box opened on her lap. She was wearing the gold locket. "But I love the locket," she said. "And I love the pretty pictures inside."

Mama came into the bedroom and sat down next to her. "I love the locket too," she said, opening it up. "And the pretty pictures are of my own mama and papa. They are all I have of them."

Leah looked at the picture of the woman who was her grandmother. She wore a blouse with a lace collar high around her neck. Her long, black hair was piled on top of her head, and her eyes were large and dark, like Leah's. Mama often told Leah that she looked just like her grandmother. Leah's grandfather had a dark beard and wore a high black skullcap.

"And I love the watch," said Esther, gently removing it from the jewelry box.

"Papa's watch," said Leah, softly. And

everyone was quiet for a moment. Even Rose, who was licking the sugar off a piece of *kichel*, stopped to look at the gold watch with the long chain that Papa always wore in his vest pocket. The watch swung back and forth, catching the late afternoon sunlight that streamed through the bedroom window.

"Please, Mama," Leah begged. "Wind it up so we can listen to it tick."

Mama carefully wound the watch, clicked open the cover, and held it to each girl's ear.

As Leah waited patiently for her turn, she glanced around the room at the wooden cabinet and chest of drawers that still held some of Papa's clothes. And at the bookcase still filled with Papa's books.

When Mama held the watch for Leah, she closed her eyes and listened to the ticking: strong and steady, like Papa was. And for a moment she was sitting on Papa's lap, listening to the watch and turning the pages while he sang to her from his siddur, his prayer book. Papa was a scholar, always learning from the holy books—often late into the night—by lamplight or candlelight.

The ticking was gone. Now Mama was holding the watch to her own ear. Leah recognized the faraway look that came to Mama's eyes whenever she thought about Papa.

Rose broke the silence with the clicking sounds she made by dropping Mama's earrings into her tea can. She spilled them out on the floor and dropped them back in again.

The clicking sounds brought Mama back from far away. She snapped the watch cover in place. "See what happens," she said to Esther. "Rose sees you play with the jewelry, and then she plays too. Soon everything will be lost or broken, and there will be nothing left.

"So"—Mama gathered up the jewelry—"we put everything back in the box, and in the drawer. And if you want to see anything, you ask me first. We will look together."

Mama reached into her apron pocket and held out her hand. "Leah, take a few kopecks and go buy six apples. Tonight we will have baked apples, and eggs from the samovar."

Mama used the samovar not only to heat up water for tea but also to make hard-boiled eggs.

Leah took the money and her sweater and started out the door. She turned around to see Esther behind her, and behind Esther, Rose.

"Mama," called Leah. "They're following me."

"Let them go with you," Mama said.

"Please, Mama, can't I go alone?"

"Another time," said Mama. "The wife of the tinsmith brought me a whole bushel of flour. I have to bake bread for her and her daughters. With so much work, it would help me if you would take Esther and Rose."

Leah let out a deep sigh as she took Esther by one hand and Rose by the other.

"Take care of each other," Mama called after them as they walked out into the street. "And get firm apples."

Mama usually got her apples from Cousin Hershel, who had a job as a guard in an apple orchard. The man who owned the orchard often gave him extra apples. And when he did, Hershel gave some of them to Mama.

But Leah liked it better when Mama ran out of apples—or tea or other food. Then Mama sent Leah to the store or to Rabbi Rubinstein's house to buy yeast. The rabbi was poor, and he sold yeast to earn extra money. Leah loved to go shopping for Mama. Especially if she could go without

Esther and Rose. It gave her a chance to be alone, to walk through the streets and look in the shop windows without worrying about her sisters lagging behind or running up ahead.

Now the scents that drifted out of the café and tea shop mingled and swirled through the air around the three girls as they walked along Walenska Street. They stopped to peer through the window of the café, to watch the rich people eating at small, round tables covered with white tablecloths and being served by a girl not much older than Leah. Some of the people stopped eating and stared back at the sisters, who then hurried away from the window and continued walking.

They passed white and gray brick houses which stood close to one another. Some of them were small, like their own. Others, like the doctor's, were large—two stories high, with balconies in front. Tucked in between the houses were a bakery and a dress shop. Even a small theater, where the girls had once seen a puppet show.

They turned the corner and walked toward the grocery store, which stood at the edge of the marketplace.

"Remember," said Leah as they entered the store, "we have to pick firm apples."

"But they'll get soft and mushy anyway, when Mama bakes them," said Esther.

"Soft and mushy is good *after* they're baked," said Leah. "Not before."

Leah loved being in the small grocery store with its sacks of flour and sugar, barrels of herring, and display cases of peppermint candy, rock candy, and Leah's favorite, *yerissen*—squares of soft chocolate-caramel candy.

She liked Mr. Abramovitz, the storekeeper, too. He had been good friends with Papa, and knew Mama and the girls well. But now Mr. Abramovitz seemed too busy to notice that the girls were there. He was leaning over a barrel of herring, muttering to himself. His long salt-and-pepper beard reached halfway down his chest. Leah was sure that if it grew any longer, it would find its way into the barrel one of these days.

The storekeeper pulled herrings out of the barrel one at a time, examined them, and dropped each one back in again. To Leah, it looked as if he were fishing. Finally he found one to his liking, took it out, and held it up to admire. Esther and Rose pinched their noses shut.

"Ah, Reb Itche's daughters," he said when he finally noticed them. "What brings you here?"

"Mama wants us to buy apples," Leah answered.

"And how is your mama?"

"She's well," said Leah.

"And working very hard, I'm sure," he said, placing the herring on the counter, on

a sheet of brown paper. He wiped his hands on his white apron. "But when it comes to baking bread, your mama is the best. She has golden hands."

Leah tried to picture Mama with golden hands, and a giggle came up through her throat.

"Time for apple picking," said Mr. Abramovitz, handing a paper bag to Leah. He found a small wooden box behind the counter and placed it on the floor in front of the apple bin. "Come on, curly head," he said to Rose, and he picked her up and lifted her onto the box so she could reach the apples easily.

Leah decided that they could each choose two apples. Esther knew exactly which apples she wanted. But every time Rose chose an apple, she showed it to Leah. "This one?" she'd ask. "This one?" Once Leah said yes, but mostly she said no. It took a long time for Rose to pick two apples that were good enough for Mama's baked apples.

After they carefully selected the six red-dest, shiniest, firmest apples they could find, Leah gave the storekeeper the money, and he reached under the wooden counter and came up with a piece of *yerissen*.

"Something for you to share," he told them. "And give regards to your mama."

Esther reached for the candy. "I'll hold it," she said.

Leah said thank you to the storekeeper. To Esther she said, "Don't eat it all up."

"I won't," said Esther. "We'll take it home and have a party."

"A party?" asked Rose. Her face bright-ened.

"There's just enough for a taste, not a party," said Leah, "but a taste is better than nothing."

The sisters walked toward home along the cobblestone street, with Rose skipping up a few feet ahead. While they were walking,

Leah glimpsed Esther nibbling on the candy.

"I thought we were saving that for home," she said, ready to take the candy away.

"We are," said Esther, who was just as quick to pull it out of Leah's reach. "I just wanted a taste of it." Then she ran ahead to be with Rose.

Leah, welcoming the chance to be alone, walked by herself for a few minutes, savoring the familiar sights and sounds of the street—shutters creaking, children playing, and storekeepers sitting in doorways on wooden boxes. Soldiers roamed about, shoppers hurried by with their sacks and bundles, water carriers moved along with their pails full. And horses made clip-clopping sounds as they pulled wagons through the streets. Leah held the moment. Then she joined Esther and Rose, who had stopped in front of the toy shop to look in the window.

Dolls of all kinds stared back at them. Some new ones, and some who were old friends. Beautiful dolls with real hair and blue glass eyes. To Leah, the most beautiful of all was a doll just like one that Marina, the doctor's daughter, had. She wore a satin dress with ruffles and a lace bonnet over her long chestnut-brown hair. She came all the way from France, Marina had told her.

Leah had a doll at home. So did Esther and Rose. Mama had made them out of cloth and yarn. They had red yarn mouths and black button eyes. Leah loved her doll. Still, whenever she could, she came here to admire these dolls. And though she never went inside and could never hope to have a doll like any of the ones she saw, she could at least come by to look in the window and dream. And in the middle of her dream this afternoon, she saw through the reflection in the window, Esther taking another nibble of candy. Leah turned around just as Esther

30

managed to slip the candy from her mouth to behind her back.

Leah gave her a "Mama look." A look without words. But one that said more than words could ever say.

And Esther understood the look. "I'm still just tasting it," she said.

"I wonder," said Leah as they continued their walk, "I wonder what kinds of dolls they have in America."

"Me too," said Esther.

"Me too," said Rose.

The lateness of the afternoon and the aromas of the tea shop and café led them toward Walenska Street and home. But the best aroma of all was the one that came from their own house as they neared the door. That aroma brought with it the promise of warm dark bread, baked apples, hard-boiled eggs, and a taste of *yerissen* for dessert.

"Mama, wait till you see the apples we picked out," said Leah, walking into the

31

kitchen. "And our special surprise dessert."

Leah looked down at Esther's hands and found them empty. "The candy," said Leah. "Where's the candy?"

Esther studied her hands as if she herself were surprised to see them empty. She looked up at Leah and shrugged.

"All gone," she said, licking her lips.

CHAPTER 4

Running from Zimmel

"Mama, come quick! Esther is in the alley, picking up pieces of glass."

Leah ran from the alley to the front of the house, where Mama was sweeping the sidewalk. "Hurry, Mama, Rose is playing with glass too."

"Glass?" cried Mama, dropping the broom. "What kind of children play with glass?"

Leah led Mama to the alley where Esther sat arranging pieces of colored glass on the ground. Rose was sitting next to her, dropping smaller pieces into her tea can.

"Esther, you get up this minute," Mama said as she took the can from Rose and shook out the pieces of glass. Rose started to cry.

"*Sha!*" said Mama. "Since when do you play with glass?"

"But the glass has such pretty colors," said Esther.

"Colors *schmullers*," said Mama. "Colored glass cuts just as bad as plain glass. And on the cold dirt you sit? Come, I give you both a bath."

Mama led Esther and Rose into the house, and Leah carried in Mama's broom. Leah then helped Mama move the tub near the oven, where it was nice and warm. She put extra wood in the oven to keep the fire going. The oven was used not just for baking but for heating the house too. It was surrounded by walls of brick, and you could even sleep on top of it in the winter.

Mama heated up pots of water on the stove. And because Zimmel was in the kitchen working at his bench, she hung a curtain in front of the tub for privacy. While she undressed Esther and Rose behind the curtain, Leah began sweeping the floor around Zimmel's chair. Zimmel was humming and sewing, and Leah was humming and sweeping.

There was always something to sweep up in Zimmel's corner—scraps of leather, thread, nails—and Leah enjoyed sweeping everything into one big pile. Leah was glad when Zimmel got up from his chair so she could move it aside and do a really good job. But without warning, Zimmel sat back down where the chair was supposed to be. Only the chair wasn't there. And *"Aaah!"* Zimmel fell on the floor, his legs shooting up in the air. Leah looked down to see him with his mouth open and with such a surprised expression, she thought his eyes would pop right out of his face. A face that was beginning to turn as red as the apples she had brought back from Mr. Abramovitz's grocery store.

Leah had never before seen Zimmel with a face the color of apples. She turned and bolted out of the house.

She fled to the park. She ran the few blocks without stopping even once to look in the shop windows. The gate was unlocked, so she went inside. And there she walked among the trees and flowers and tried to forget about Zimmel. But she could not forget. She kept seeing him on the floor with his legs up in the air and his red face and his bulging eyes. She hoped he wasn't hurt. And she hoped he wouldn't yell at her when she went back. Zimmel had never yelled before, but she had never spilled him onto the floor before either.

Leah sat down on a bench and watched the leaves skipping along the path. She put

her hands in the pockets of her sweater, to warm them, and found her pencil and her unfinished letter to Cousin Ruth. She continued writing.

I am in the park now, and the leaves are playing tag in the wind. I wish you could see how beautiful it is here. There are trees and flowers all around. In the middle of the park, there is a small bridge, with water on both sides. The hills are beyond, and on one hill there is a beautiful house that looks like a palace. I think a very rich and important family must live there. At night the gate to the park is locked.

Leah went on to write about Esther and the glass and how Mama was giving Esther and Rose a bath next to the oven, where it was warm. Thoughts of Zimmel came to mind, but she quickly pushed them aside. She wrote about the weather turning colder.

Soon we will be sleeping next to the oven.
And when it gets very, very cold outside, we
will take turns sleeping on top of the oven.

She also told how Esther tried to escape
from the imaginary soldiers by climbing in
through the window. *Are there soldiers in
America?* Leah wanted to know. *And do they
break into your house to steal from you?*

Leah wrote until she was all out of paper.
But it didn't matter. She had to go home
anyway. It was time. Maybe Zimmel
wouldn't yell at her. He hadn't yelled when
she and Esther and Rose took turns wearing
the new shoes he had just finished making
for the rabbi. He hadn't yelled when they
used his shoe polish to paint their finger-
nails. And after all, Leah hadn't made him
fall on purpose, had she?

The more she thought about it, the more
certain she became that Zimmel would not
yell. That he would forgive her.

40

Leah folded the letter and carefully put it in her pocket. Tomorrow she would mail it at the post office on Studentska Street. She got up from the bench, wrapped her sweater around herself, and joined the leaves in their game of tag.

CHAPTER 5

The Parade

"Mama, come quick! Esther has nails in her mouth."

Leah ran to the kitchen table, where Mama was drinking tea with the butcher's wife.

"Nails?" cried Mama. "She has nails in her mouth?"

"She looks like Zimmel," said Rose, who was following right behind Leah.

Mama got up quickly and hurried over to

Esther, who was sitting in Zimmel's chair, taking nails out of her mouth one at a time, and pounding them into his workbench.

"Hold still and don't say a word," said Mama, removing the nails from Esther's mouth one by one. "You must never, never do this again."

"But Zimmel always has nails in his mouth," said Esther.

"Zimmel is a shoemaker. You are a little girl," Mama answered. She took Esther by the hand and led her to the table, where she broke off a piece of bread. "Here, you put bread in your mouth. Not nails. When Zimmel comes back from delivering shoes, he will not be happy to find nails in his bench."

The butcher's wife gave Esther a disapproving look, shook her head, and made *tsk tsk* sounds with her tongue. She was the nosiest person Leah knew. Everyone said she was the nosiest person in Nesvich. Leah thought she was probably the nosiest person in all of Russia. She had a thin face and birdlike eyes. The rest of her was plump. Leah thought she looked like one of the butcher's chickens.

The butcher's wife took a sip of tea. "In America they have white bread," she said, after she swallowed. "Can you imagine that? It's true. My uncle Velvl wrote to me from America about it. They have bread as white as the snow."

Leah listened with interest. In her next letter, she would have to remember to ask the cousins if it was true about the white bread. The only bread she knew of was brown, except for the challah, the twisted loaves of Sabbath bread, which was a golden yellow.

The conversation then switched from bread to the butcher. His wife was complaining that he spent too much time talking to his customers.

"Anna, I'm telling you. All of a sudden

he thinks he's a chef. Every time he sells a piece of meat, he thinks he has to give a recipe to go with it."

The two women began to exchange recipes, and Leah turned her attention to Papa's black umbrella, which was kept in a corner of the kitchen. She opened it up and with the umbrella over her head, she began twirling around the kitchen, humming to herself. She twirled and twirled, pretending she was a beautiful, famous dancer, performing on a grand stage. She spun around until a voice pierced her spinning and broke the mood.

"The child should not open an umbrella in the house. She will have bad luck."

It was the butcher's wife. Leah came to a stop and steadied herself against a chair, waiting for the room to stop spinning.

"You remember Mrs. Moskowitz from the fish store? Once she opened an umbrella in her house, and six months later all her teeth fell out."

"So?" said Mama. "Maybe she had bad teeth."

"No, no," insisted the butcher's wife. "It was because of the umbrella."

"Leahla," Mama said, "put the umbrella away."

"But Mama . . ."

"You will have bad luck," said the butcher's wife.

"Fat cow," Leah whispered as she closed the umbrella. But the whisper came out louder than Leah expected.

There was a sudden silence. Mama and the butcher's wife stared at her. So did Esther and Rose. They were staring, and their mouths were open. Leah felt her face grow hot. She dropped the umbrella, and for the second time in a week, she ran out of the house.

She ran in the direction of the park, away from the butcher's wife, away from Mama and the spanking that would surely be waiting for her.

Music was coming from the park, and Leah hurried toward it. The organ grinder and his monkey were just outside the gate. And from inside the park came the sounds of drums and horns and crashing cymbals. Leah pushed through the crowd of townspeople and soldiers and, to her delight, saw a parade starting up.

Why would there be a parade? Leah wondered. Maybe it was to welcome an important person who had come to town. But before she could give any more thought to the reason, the marching began. From all sides, people hurried to follow the band. She recognized some of her neighbors. The tinsmith's wife was there with her two daughters. From afar she saw Marina and waved to her. Then the next thing she knew, Leah was being swept along with everyone, and she too became part of the parade.

They marched around the park, past the fountain, and over the bridge. Leah had seen parades before but never had she been part of one. She marched along, the music tugging at her and sending wonderful little shivers through her body. Oh, how exciting! This was much more fun than dancing with an umbrella.

Leah was thoroughly caught up in the music and magic of this moment as she blew imaginary horns and beat imaginary drums. She was so caught up that she didn't even notice the people leaving and the music growing fainter and fainter, until there was no music at all. When she finally looked around, she saw that there was no parade, no people, nothing. Just Leah herself, all alone at the edge of an apple orchard.

"Where did everyone go?" she asked out loud. But no one answered her. A little cry came up from deep inside. "Lost," she said. "I'm lost."

She wrapped her sweater around herself and looked up into the trees. The tree trunks wore faces with mean eyes and angry

mouths. Was this the bad luck the butcher's wife had warned her about? Is this what comes from opening an umbrella in the house?

Leah turned away from the trees and looked down at the ground. An apple was lying near her feet. She thought about picking it up but decided against it. They would arrest her for stealing. Leah didn't want to go to jail.

A few months ago, Mama had gone to jail. Once, just after she had finished sweeping the street, a horse came along and dirtied it. There was a law that said you had to keep the street in front of your house clean. Otherwise you had to pay a fine. Leah thought the law was unfair. Mama always tried her best to keep the street clean. But when it comes to horses, you never can tell when they're going to pass by and dirty it again. Was it Mama's fault that one came by when she wasn't looking? Was it Mama's fault that she didn't have enough money to pay the fine?

So they put her in jail for one day. Mama was allowed to pick the day. She chose Saturday, the Sabbath, the day of rest, so she wouldn't have to miss out on a day of work. The tinsmith's wife had looked after the girls for a few hours. Then Leah, Esther, and Rose had gone to visit Mama. They stayed with her until nightfall, in a small room that had no windows—just a table and a few chairs. They sat by candlelight the whole time, with nothing to do.

Thinking of jails and stealing made Leah think of something else too. One summer when Cousin Hershel had to guard the apple orchard, he had taken Leah with him. She had spent the night under the stars, helping Hershel—when she wasn't curled up in a blanket, sleeping—guard the orchard from thieves. Could it be, Leah wondered, that this was the same orchard?

She answered the question almost before

she asked it. This had to be the same orchard. After all, wasn't the fence that surrounded it half-black and half-red? Just like the fence that surrounded the orchard that she and Hershel had guarded?

"Hershel," she had asked that evening, "is this a red fence waiting to be painted black or a black fence waiting to be painted red?"

And Hershel had answered, "The fence hasn't decided yet."

Leah walked along the fence for several feet, and sure enough, just where black met red, there was a road that looked like the one she and Hershel had taken home. Leah ran like the wind, down the road and through the woods. This had to be the right road. It just had to be. But what if it wasn't? What if there were other fences painted black and red?

Leah tried not to think about that. And she tried not to look at the tree-trunk faces that whizzed by. Faces that were ready to jump right out at her if she so much as glanced at them. Birds screeched overhead, and she was sure they were giant birds that would sweep down and carry her away.

She kept her eyes straight ahead as she ran, until finally she saw a clearing. And beyond the clearing was a town. Her town! There was the park and the bridge and the house that looked like a palace.

"Oh, beautiful Nesvich," Leah called as she ran through the streets toward home, past the theater, the café, and the tea shop.

And there at 15 Walenska Street was her house. "Oh, beautiful house." She hugged the door. It was so good to be back.

And maybe Mama would forget about the spanking.

But Mama didn't forget. Mama never forgot. Leah didn't care. She was home. Home where it was safe.

CHAPTER 6

The Soldiers Are Coming

"Children, come quick! The soldiers are coming!"

Mama ran into the house and shut the door behind her. She hurried to the bedroom to gather up Leah, Esther, and Rose. Then she led them to the secret door in the floor that opened to the cellar. Papa had once attached a rug over the door so the soldiers wouldn't know about the cellar.

"There is talk all over the neighborhood,"

said Mama. "The soldiers are coming to make an investigation."

Leah understood what Mama was talking about. The soldiers went from house to house to investigate what you had, and if they saw something they wanted, they took it from you. The way they had taken Papa's wine cup and Mama's candlesticks.

"Hurry, now," Mama said, reaching under the rug and lifting the door. "Go down and be quiet."

Leah suddenly remembered Zimmel. They needed him to protect them. He needed them too. "Mama, where is Zimmel?"

"In another town. Delivering shoes. Now go."

Esther helped Rose down the narrow ladder while Leah watched Mama hide the jewelry in the oven. Then Mama did something that Leah had never seen her do before. From a shelf she took loaves of bread and honey cake that she had baked earlier that day and spread them out on the kitchen table.

Why was Mama doing this? But there was no time to ask. With Mama following close behind, Leah too went down into the cold dirt cellar where extra sacks of flour, potatoes, and Hershel's apples were kept.

Mama closed the door above them, and they all huddled together in the dark, on the flour sacks, waiting for the soldiers. They huddled in the damp cellar for a long time, and just when they thought the soldiers weren't coming, they heard a banging on the kitchen door. "You in there. Open up!"

The door slammed open, and heavy footsteps stomped across the floor above them. Mama drew her girls closer, and they all held one another. Then came the sounds of furniture being thrown over and glass breaking.

"Papa," Esther cried. "I want Papa."
Rose let out a whimper.

Mama hushed them both. "*Shh*, it will be all right."

Leah wanted Papa too. He had always been with them during these investigations, and she had felt safe with his strong arms around her. Leah was used to seeing the soldiers in their brown uniforms outside in the streets, but it scared her to have them stomping into her house and stealing from them.

There were more footsteps overhead. This time closer, stopping directly over the secret door. Rose buried her face in Mama's chest. No one moved. No one breathed.

Finally, the footsteps strode away. There was talking. Even some laughter. A door slammed. Then silence. Mama and the girls waited there, frozen in place. Then Mama crept upstairs, pushed open the door, and looked around.

"They are gone," she said, and guided the children up the steps. They were shocked to see what had happened to the little house that Mama always kept so neat and clean. Chairs and tables were overturned. Drawers had been emptied, their contents thrown all over the floor: clothes and the letters from America; colored stones and pebbles that the girls had collected at the park and lake; even the little dolls that Mama had made for them.

Rose's tea can was bent at the lid. And some of Mama's dishes were broken. But worst of all, Papa's holy books were scattered on the floor, many with their bindings crushed and pages torn.

They stared in silence at the sight before them, and then began the task of putting the little room back together. They lovingly picked up each one of Papa's books, kissed it, and placed it on the shelves. Mama swept up the pieces of broken dishes and put the kitchen in order, while Leah, Esther, and Rose straightened the chairs and returned everything to the drawers. That's when they heard Mama crying. No, it was more like the sound of Mama laughing.

"Why are you laughing, Mama?" Leah asked.

"I am so happy the soldiers like the way I bake." Mama was standing at the kitchen table. "Look, they took all the bread and cake."

Leah glanced at the kitchen table. It was true. There was not one loaf of bread or honey cake left. Why would Mama be happy about that? Esther and Rose looked puzzled too.

"Soldiers do not like to leave a house with empty hands," Mama explained. "They get angry. I just made sure to let them leave with their arms full." She laughed again, and this time the girls did too.

"Poor Zimmel," said Esther. "He's far away, and missing all the excitement."

"This kind of excitement we don't need," said Mama.

When everything was back in order, it looked to Leah as if the soldiers had never been there.

"Come," said Mama. "Let us go and see if the neighbors need help. And then I must get back to my baking."

Mama and the sisters went from house to house, looking in on their friends, helping whenever they could, or just sitting and talking and being grateful that no one had been hurt. Only at the butcher's house did Leah wait outside. Ever since she had called his wife a fat cow, she tried to stay away from her. But she cared about her. She didn't want her to be hurt.

"How is everyone?" Leah asked, when Mama and the girls came out of the butcher's house.

63

"They are fine, thank God," said Mama.

"But the butcher's wife is angry," said Esther. "The soldiers stole her umbrella."

Leah and Esther were both overcome by a fit of giggles. Leah thought she saw a smile on Mama's face.

When they were satisfied that all their neighbors were safe, Mama and the girls went back home. But as soon as they stepped into the house, they knew that something was wrong. An odd smell greeted them from the kitchen.

"Oh, no!" cried Mama, rushing to the oven. "How could I have forgotten?"

Mama grabbed a towel and opened the oven door. She pulled out strange-looking clumps of melted metal. Slowly the girls began to recognize the misshapen pieces of familiar objects. They found themselves staring at what was once Mama's jewelry: earrings, necklaces, and to their horror, Papa's watch. Mama leaned against the table and sank into a chair.

"How could I have done such a thing? To light the oven and forget the jewelry. Now there is nothing left." Mama's eyes filled with tears.

When Leah saw Mama crying, she too began to cry. Then Esther cried. And Rose cried with them.

Quickly Mama wiped her eyes. Then she went around wiping the eyes of her daughters. "We must not cry," she said. "The jewelry is not what matters. What matters is that we have one another and we are all safe. That is what Papa always said, remember? Now, come. Let us bake bread."

"Mama, come quick! Really quick!" Leah was calling from the bedroom.

"Leah, where's the fire? I'm moving as fast as I can." Mama pulled away the bedroom curtain to see Leah, Esther, and Rose standing there, grinning.

"Surprise, Mama," said Rose. "See what Esther is wearing?"

Mama looked at Esther in her underwear. She could not believe what she saw around Esther's neck. "The locket? You have the locket?"

"Yes, Mama," said Leah. "The locket with the pictures of your own mama and papa."

"But how . . . ? Where . . . ?"

"I put the locket on before I got dressed," said Esther, "and I forgot all about it."

Mama buried her head in her hands. The sisters couldn't tell if she was laughing or crying. Then Mama looked up at Esther. "*Oy*, Estherla, Estherla, for once I am glad you did not listen to your mama." She hugged her.

"But what about Papa?" asked Leah, remembering the watch. "You still have nothing left of Papa."

"Papa's books," said Esther.

"Ah, I do have something left of Papa,"

Mama said. "And something even better than the books." She gathered Leah, Esther, and Rose in her arms.

"I have you."

CHAPTER 7

The Letter
from America

"Leah, come quick! The letter from America."

Esther was out in front of the house, jumping up and down and waving a white envelope.

Leah, who was on her way back from buying yeast from the rabbi, ran toward the house as soon as she saw what Esther had in her hand.

"Finally, it's here," she called out as she

ran. Leah had mailed her letter in the fall, and now it was almost spring.

"Hurry, Leah. Everyone is waiting."

Everyone was Mama, Rose, Zimmel, and the butcher's wife—who by this time seemed to have forgiven Leah for her remark. They were sitting around the kitchen table, eating some of Mama's honey cake and drinking tea out of glasses.

"Come, Leahla," said Mama, patting the chair next to her. "Read us the letter. Tell us about the cousins."

"I wonder," interrupted the butcher's wife, "if your cousins know my uncle Velvl."

"America is a big place," offered Zimmel, breaking off a piece of honey cake. His fingers bore faint stains from black shoe polish.

"It's still a small world," the butcher's wife continued. "When my uncle Velvl went over, who should he meet but Shmulke the

tailor, who used to live right here on Walenska Street."

"They met because they both went to
the same city. But these cousins live in
Minnesota, and your uncle lives in New
York."

"Enough, already," said Mama, waving a
hand at them. "Let her read."

But Leah wasn't ready to read the letter.
First she had to study the envelope with
the foreign postmark and stamp, printed in
English. An envelope that had come by boat
from very far away. And it had Leah's name
written right on the front.

Leah very carefully and neatly tore open
the flap of the envelope and pulled out the
sheet of paper. She knew she would be
reading this letter over and over. Not just
to herself but to some of the other neighbors
too. It was not often that a letter from
America came to Walenska Street, but when
it did, they all wanted to share it.

Rose crawled onto Mama's lap as Leah began reading in Yiddish:

Dear Aunt Anna, Leah, Esther, and Rose,

At the mention of their names, they smiled.

We were all happy to hear from you and thank God that you are well. We feel good knowing that Zimmel is with you.

Upon hearing his name, Zimmel smiled too. Leah went on to read news of the family and the cold Minnesota weather, which reminded them of Russia. And then Ruth answered some of Leah's questions:

Leah, you are almost right about the curtains. They are yellow. And in the early morning, the sun touches them with small white circles that look just like flowers.

Leah glanced up from her letter. "I knew it," she whispered to herself.

We have soldiers in America too. But they are here to protect the people. And they do not break into our houses to steal from us or hurt us.

There are all kinds of good things to eat in America. You would love bananas.

Leah looked up. "Bananas?" she repeated. And everyone shrugged, puzzled by the meaning of the word.

A banana is a narrow and curved fruit that is soft and creamy and sweet. It's covered with a yellow skin that you peel off with your fingers.

"Mmmm," said Esther.
"Mmmm," said Rose.

Mama, Zimmel, and the butcher's wife, nodded as if they now understood. Leah tried to imagine such a fruit. Maybe in her next letter she would ask Ruth to draw her a picture of it.

Ruth also wrote about some things called hot dogs and ice cream and explained what they were.

Maybe, God willing, one day you will all come to America and see everything for yourselves.

Leah stopped reading. There was silence in the kitchen, and everyone seemed to savor those last words.

"They need shoemakers in America too," said Zimmel.

"In America they also need butchers," said the butcher's wife. "Butchers with recipes, yet."

"Maybe in America I won't have to bake bread," said Mama.

Maybe one day you will come to America
and see everything for yourselves.

"Do you think so, Mama?" Leah asked.
"Do you think one day we'll go to America?"

"If it is meant to be," Mama answered.

"I would like to go to America," said Esther.

"Me too," said Rose.

It was a beautiful-sounding name, *America*. It had to be a beautiful place. Leah tried to picture what it would look like. Lots of trees and grass, probably. Very blue skies. A place where people smiled a lot. So many dolls that every girl could have one with a satin dress and lace bonnet. And strange-looking fruit called bananas.

"Look at us," said Mama, laughing. "One letter and we are all off to America. Finish reading, Leah. Enough dreaming for one day. And then all of you"—she motioned to her three girls—"go to the park and play. It is too nice to be inside."

Leah read the rest of the letter and handed it back to Mama. Mama studied it and ran her fingers across the words, before passing the letter around for everyone to look at. Then Leah took Esther by one hand and Rose by the other, and the three sisters stepped out onto Walenska Street.

Leah would go to the park and play, but she would dream there too. For Leah, there would always be more dreams.

This photograph, taken in 1913 in Nesvich, Russia, was the inspiration for *The House on Walenska Street*. It shows the author's grandmother and grandfather, and (from left to right) her aunts Rose and Esther, and her mother, Leah.

Temple Israel
Minneapolis, Minnesota

IN HONOR OF
THE 40TH WEDDING ANNIVERSARY OF
DR. & MRS. EVERETT PERLMAN
FROM
JOANNE & BRUCE BLINDMAN